Introducing Lydia Monks . . .

I don't like spiders!
Why do they have to live in houses?
I think they should all live happily in the garden . . .
preferably in someone ELSE'S garden!

Why can't spiders get the message? . . .
No one LIKES them!

Lydia

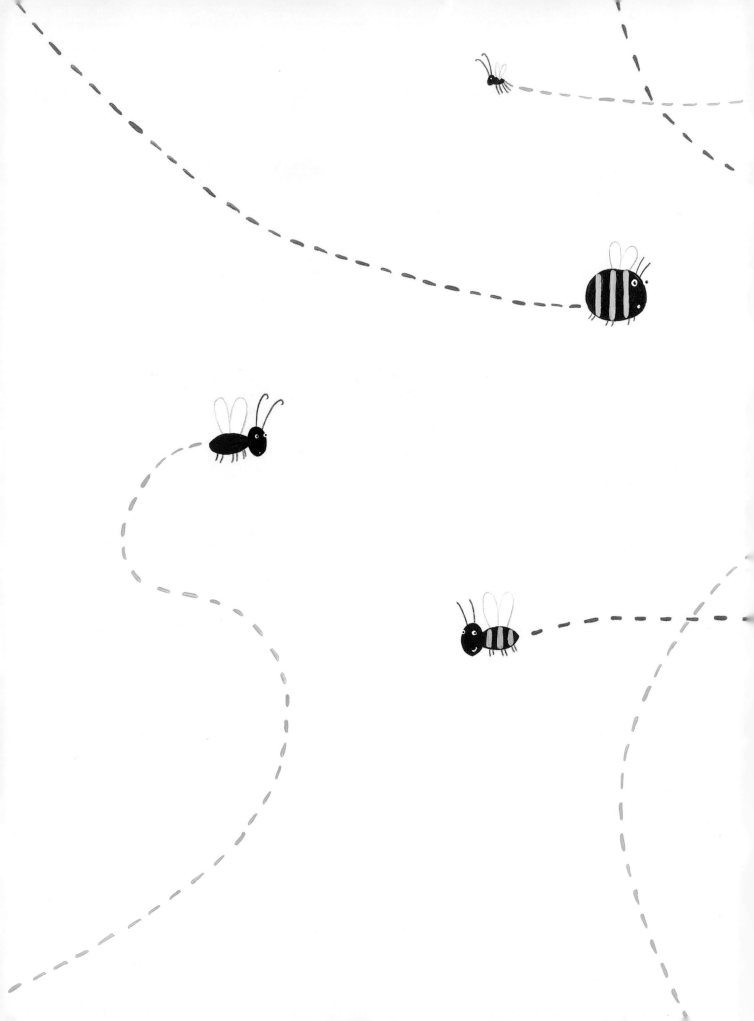

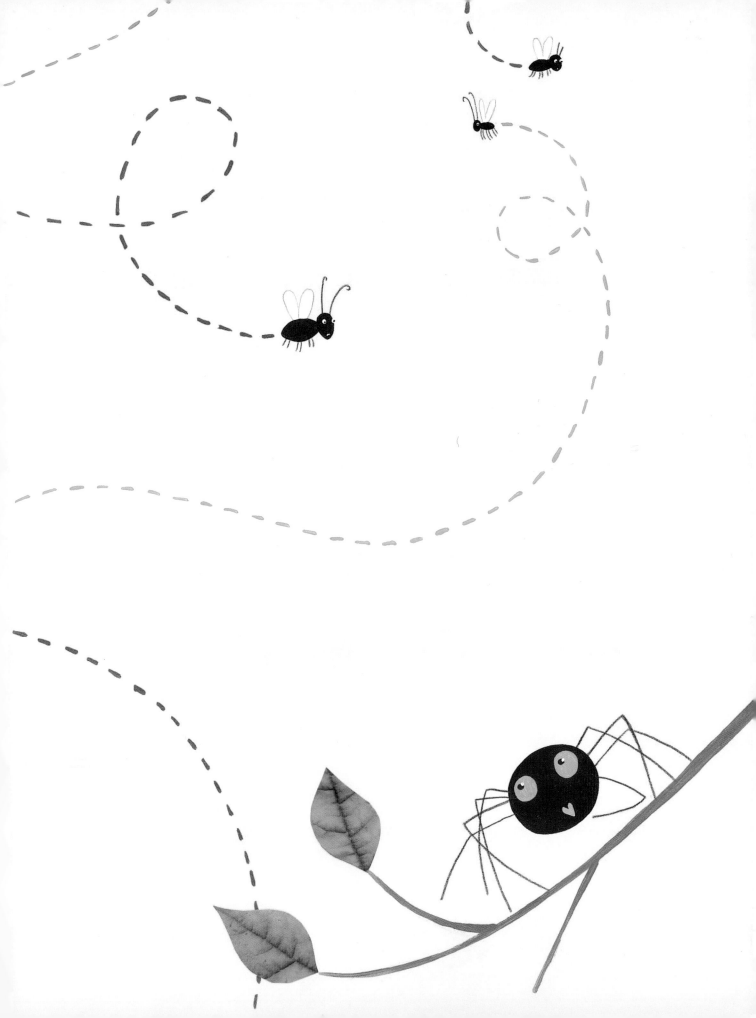

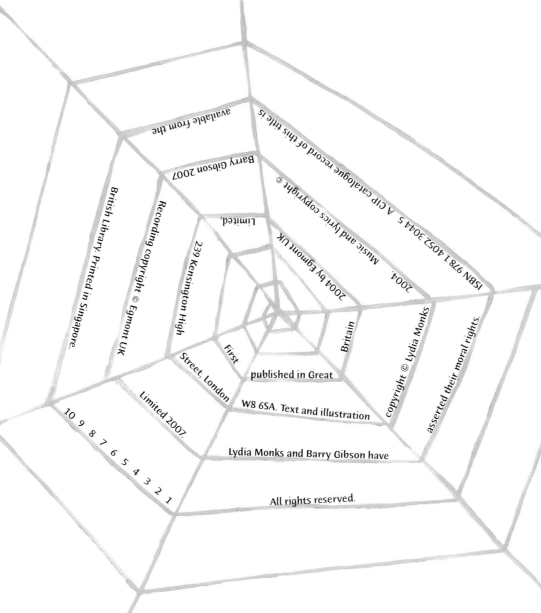

available from the

British Library. A CIP catalogue record of this title is

ISBN 978 1 4052 3044 5

Barry Gibson 2007

2004. Music and lyrics copyright ©

Recording copyright © Egmont UK

Limited,

copyright © Lydia Monks

239 Kensington High

2004 by Egmont UK

British Library. Printed in Singapore.

First

Street, London

Britain

asserted their moral rights.

Limited 2007.

published in Great

10 9 8 7 6 5 4 3 2 1

W8 6SA. Text and illustration

Lydia Monks and Barry Gibson have

for Marcus

Aaaarrrggghh, Spider!

Lydia Monks

EGMONT

It's really lonely
being a spider.
I want to be a
family pet.

THIS
family's pet!

I know!
I'll show them what a great dancer I am.
None of their pets can dance like me!

"Aaaarrgghh, SPIDER!"

Oh dear!

I know!
I'll show them
how clean
I am.

None of their
pets are clean
like me!

"Out

you

go!"

Oh dear!

I know!
I'll show them how easy
I am to look after.

None of their
pets can feed
themselves
like I can!

"Out

you

go!"

It's no good.
This family will
never want me.

I'm going to go
and live all alone . . .

. . . in the garden.

Look at me! Watch me ride!

Look at me! Watch me shop!

Look at me! Watch me swing!

I'm a real, true, proper pet!

In fact, I'm so happy with my new family,
I think I'll introduce them to all my friends . . .

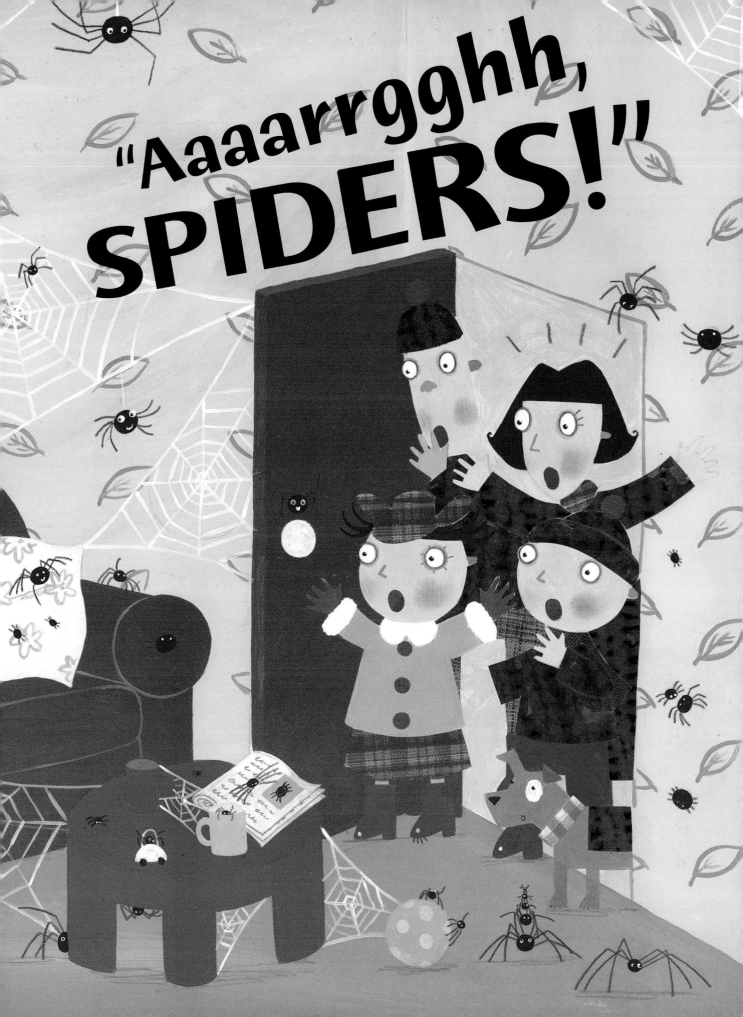

MORE WILD AND WACKY BOOKS BY

MORE BOOK AND CD FUN

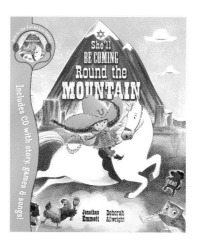